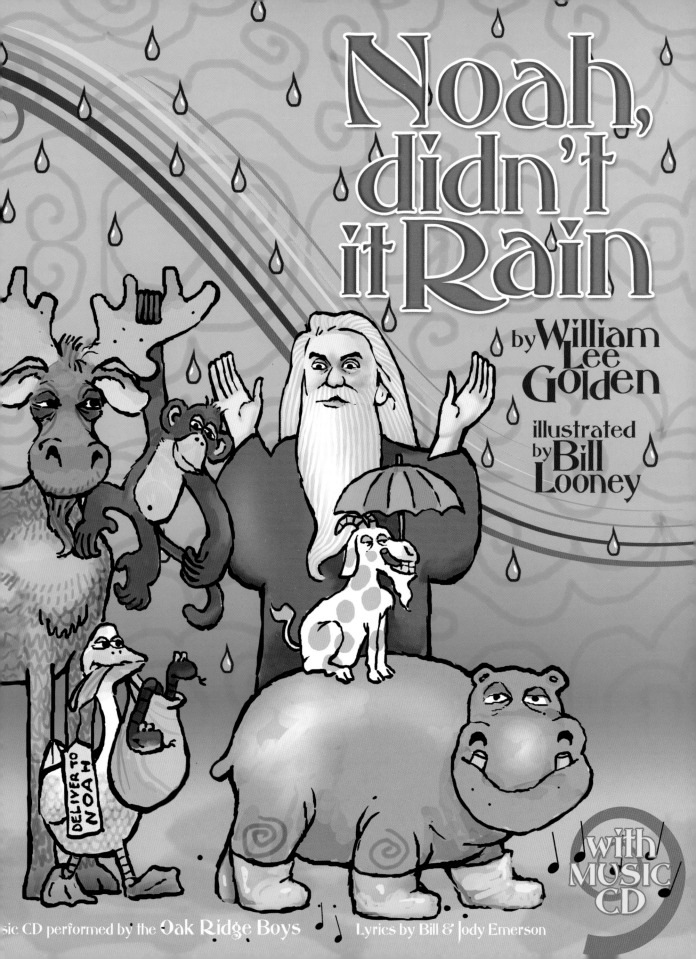

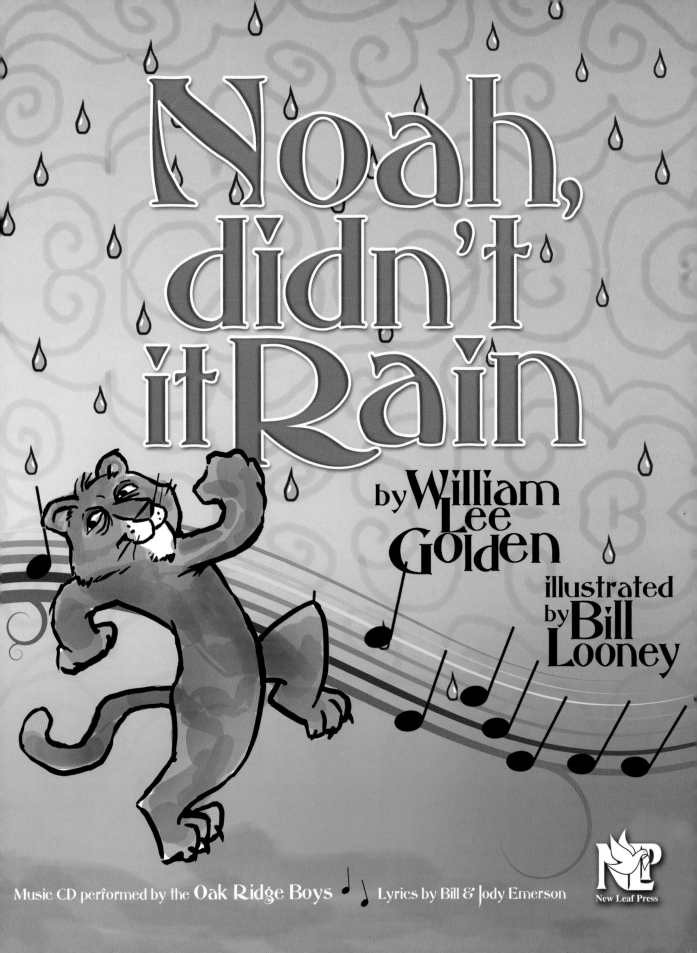

Printed in China

For information write:
New Leaf Press
P.O. Box 726
Green Forest, AR 72638

Please visit our website for
other great titles: www.nlpg.com

ISBN 13: 978-0-89221-683-3
ISBN 10: 0-89221-683-2

Library of Congress Number:
2008921036

Didn't It Rain
Song Lyrics Written by
Bill and Jody Emerson
Copyright © 2006 William Lee Golden
Music, PocoRhythm (BMI). All Rights
Reserved. International Copyright
Secured. Used By Permission. William
Lee Golden Music administered by
Copyright Solutions, P.O. Box 3390,
Brentwood TN 37024.

Narration read by William Lee Golden
www.williamleegolden.com

Producer of Record
Michael Sykes and Duane Allen

Provided courtesy of Spring Hill Music
Group, Inc.℗ "Didn't It Rain"

Story Narration Production by Flavil
Q. Van Dyke and William Lee Golden

Engineering by Ron Fairchild

dedication:

I thank God for His continued guidance and protection. He has helped me stay afloat through many floods and storms in my life. I would like to dedicate this book to my young son, Solomon, who has been singing "Didn't It Rain" since he was a toddler.

I have been a fan of Wild Bill Emerson's and his wife, Miss Jody's songwriting for many years. I thank Bill for pitching this song to me several years ago. It has stayed fresh in my mind since that first day he sang it in our home.

I would also like to thank Larry Jones and the "Feed The Children" organization for all the hard work they do unto the least. May God continue to bless and keep you.

My partners, Joe Bonsall, Richard Sterban, and Duane Allen, I thank you for your friendship. None of us would be where we are today without the Lord's guidance to put us with the greatest manager, Jim Halsey.

To the readers of this book, may you always remember to follow God's leadership and guidance on your voyage.

William Lee Golden
www.williamleegolden.com

5

The good Lord went to Noah and He told him about the flood. He said, "Noah, build Me a boat and make it out of gopher wood."

GOPHER WOOD FOREST

So that's how Noah built God a masterpiece and he called it Noah's Ark.

9

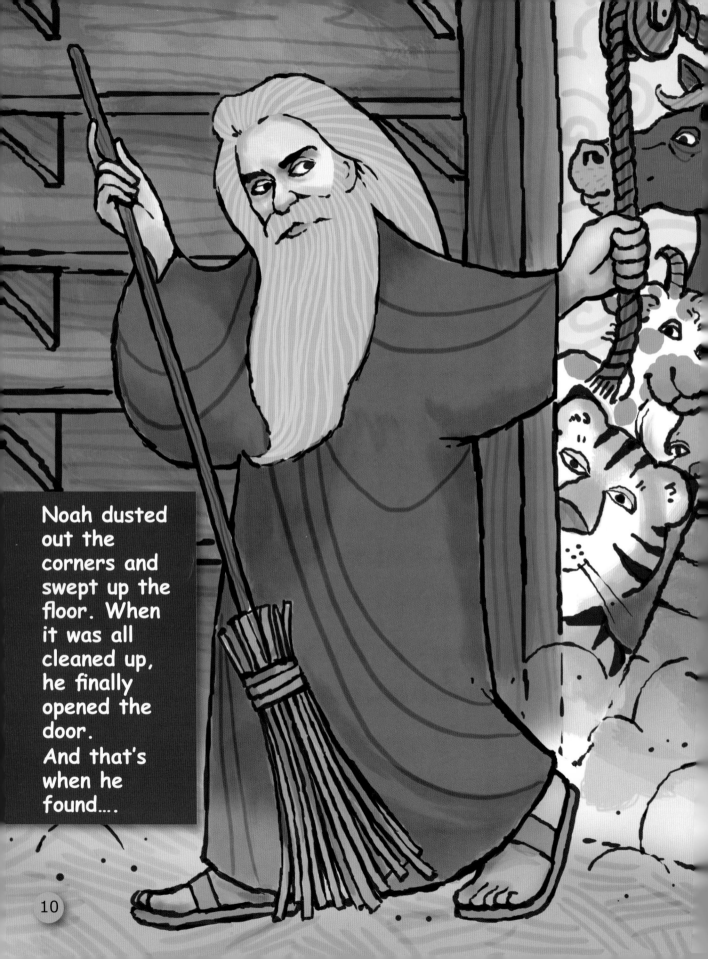

Noah dusted out the corners and swept up the floor. When it was all cleaned up, he finally opened the door.
And that's when he found....

He had
a moose,
a goose and
a gander,
an alligator,
and a
big hippo,
A monkey
and an
ape and a
couple of
snakes,
a ram, a
sheep, and
a goat.

11

He had an opossum, a raccoon and a black baboon, an eagle and a red-tailed hawk...

a buck and a doe, a turkey and a crow, and a donkey refusing to walk.

Then came the leopards, lions, and tigers, a bull and a shaggy buffalo,

Orangutans and little bitty scary things — all lined up neatly in a row.

15

Noah threw down his broom and rushed to make room.

16

"Hurry," he said as nearer they came, "there isn't much time! Soon God will send rain."

The apples, peaches, and pears,
Noah put under the stairs.
On the shelves were the pots
of grapes, plums, and apricots!

He also stored peas and beans,
squash and sweet turnip greens!

Carrots and pumpkins
stacked on the floor,
with corn, tomatoes,
and more.

He had
all the
food the
animals
would
need.

And before
God closed the
Ark's door,
Noah grabbed a
bag of mustard seed!

Didn't it rain children
Didn't it rain, rain, rain

Forty days and nights
didn't it rain.

Lord, Lord!

Forty days and nights
didn't it rain.

Left at the end were the
sky and the sea, above
and below both blue
as can be.

The Ark drifted along,
all inside having nothing
to fear, as they waited
for the water to at last
disappear.

When it was time Noah opened the door. Away went the hawk, and the bear and the boar. The eagle took wing, scattering little bitty things, along with the buck and doe and the big buffalo. The goat fell asleep trying to follow the sheep, and the snakes wiggled under a leaf.

Noah also set loose the moose and the goose, the raccoon and baboon, the hippo and crow.

Soon the Ark was empty...and then in the sky appeared a great, big rainbow. And God said "I put my rainbow in the clouds. It will help you remember my promise to you and all the animals of the earth!" (Gen. 9:13)

Now when you see rain falling, and puddles appear, think of Noah's story and remember God's love — He holds each of us near.

William Lee Golden

Entertainer • Historian • Painter

Perhaps best known as the outstanding baritone voice of the legendary Oak Ridge Boys, William Lee Golden's impressive talents range broadly. His music is recognized the world over. His contributions to history and Native American understanding have earned noteworthy awards and continuing appreciation. And, in recent years, he is making a distinctive mark in publishing and in fine art, rendering paintings of beauty and uniqueness. Visible with his long beard and flowing hair, he is one of the most recognized personalities in Country and Gospel music — the renowned "Mountain Man of Music."

The Oak Ridge Boys are known wherever music is appreciated. Gold and platinum recordings abound — 37 hits! Add to that: five Grammy Awards, one American Music Award, four Country Music Association Awards, four Academy of Country Music Awards, eight Dove Awards, and induction in the Gospel Music Hall of Fame along with numerous international acknowledgements. Among their memorable recordings are: "Thank God for Kids," "American Made," "Ozark Mountain Jubilee," and the one everyone hums, the celebrated, "Elvira."

The music developed early in William Lee Golden. In the small town of Brewton,

Alabama, this farmer's son was performing at age seven on his grandfather's weekly radio show along with his sister, Lanette, Increasingly, he was being asked to sing on stage. It was clear early on what he wanted to do — he wanted to entertain. And, has he ever! In 1997, he was inducted into the Alabama Music Hall of Fame and presented with their "Lifework Award for Performing Achievement." Reared in the arts, his love and respect for culture continues and grows to this day. His mother, Ruth, is a recognized poet, with two published volumes of inspiring poems.

William Lee Golden has always seen God's handwriting in the world. "Traveling over 160 days each year," he says, "I get to see the beauty and majesty of our country. My camera is always clicking. In recent years, I have taken a brush and easel along, and try to capture the splendorous vistas as I see them." As a student and collector, Golden has had a life-long appreciation for art. Critics and collectors commend his exceptional vision and distinctive approach to color and light. "His paintings are joyful and uplifting," says a collector. An example is the Maine coast, which he has captured in several renderings of Walker's Point, the home of former First Lady, Barbara, and President George H.W. Bush in Kennebunkport.

William Lee, Brenda, and son, Solomon, live in
Hendersonville, Tennessee in a historic home,
The "Golden Era Plantation," built in 1786. Over
the years his older sons Rusty, Craig, and Chris,
his six grandchildren and many friends have
enjoyed this "peaceful home," which Golden
feels, "encourages relaxation and creativity."

For further information about William Lee
Golden, including his new line of merchandise
and art, contact: www.williamleegolden.com.